40982

W9-BAK-505

BUTTERFIELD SCHOOL LIBRARY
1441 W. Lake Street
Libertyville, Illinois 60048

DEMCO

Happy Birthday, Eeyore!

Disney's
Winnie the Pooh First Readers

Pooh Gets Stuck
Bounce, Tigger, Bounce!
Pooh's Pumpkin
Rabbit Gets Lost
Pooh's Honey Tree
Happy Birthday, Eeyore!
Pooh's Best Friend

DISNEP'S

A Winnie the Pooh First Reader

Happy Birthday, Eeyore!

Adapted by Isabel Gaines

ILLUSTRATED BY Studio Orlando

BUTTERFIELD SCHOOL LIBRARY
1441 W. Lake Street
Libertyville, Illinois 60048

DISNEP
PRESS

NEW YORK

© 1998 by Disney Enterprises, Inc.

All rights reserved. No part of this book may be reproduced or transmitted in any form or by any means, electronic or mechanical, including photocopying, recording, or by any information storage and retrieval system, without written permission from the publisher. For information address Disney Press, 114 Fifth Avenue, New York, New York 10011-5690.

Based on the Pooh stories by A. A. Milne
(copyright The Pooh Properties Trust).

Printed in the United States of America.

First Edition

1 3 5 7 9 10 8 6 4 2

Library of Congress Catalog Card Number: 98-84027

ISBN: 0-7868-4183-4 (paperback)

For more Disney Press fun, visit www.DisneyBooks.com

Happy Birthday, Eeyore!

Eeyore was in his sad spot
when Pooh stopped by.

"Eeyore, why are you
so sad?" Pooh asked.

"It's my birthday," said Eeyore.

"Your birthday?" asked Pooh.

"Of course," said Eeyore.

"Can't you see the presents?"

Pooh looked around.

"No," said Pooh.

"The cake and candles?"
asked Eeyore.

"Well, no," said Pooh.

"Neither can I," Eeyore said sadly.

That gave Pooh an idea.

He said, "Eeyore,

wait right here."

Pooh ran to his house.

Piglet was there

looking for him.

"I must get

poor Eeyore a present,"

Pooh said. "But what?"

Pooh looked
around his house.

He saw a small
honeypot
on his shelf.
"Of course!
Honey!"
cried Pooh.
"Piglet, what are you
giving Eeyore?"
"Well, I could give him
my red balloon,"
Piglet said.

"Good idea," Pooh said.
Piglet went home
to find the balloon.
Pooh left to give
Eeyore his present.

Pooh had not gone far
when he felt strange.
It was as if someone
inside him said,
"Time to eat."

Pooh sat down
and ate the honey
in the honeypot.
He ate and ate.

When he had licked
the last sticky drop,
Pooh asked, "Now, where was
I going?

19

"Oh yes—to Eeyore's.
Oh bother! Now what
will I give Eeyore?"
Pooh began to think.

"I know!" said Pooh.

"A honeypot without honey

is a *useful* pot.

Eeyore can put whatever

he wants in it."

At the same time, Piglet carried
a red balloon to Eeyore.
"Hello, Piglet!" he heard
from above.

Piglet looked up.

Owl was flying over him.

Piglet did not see
the tree in his path.

POP! Piglet crashed

into the tree.

"Oh d-d-d-dear," said Piglet.

"The balloon broke."

25

BUTTERFIELD SCHOOL LIBRARY
1441 W. Lake Street
Libertyville, Illinois 60048

Piglet arrived
at Eeyore's house.
"Eeyore, here is
a birthday present
for you."

Piglet handed
the broken red balloon
to Eeyore.

Eeyore sadly looked
at the shredded red balloon.
Then Pooh arrived.

"I've brought you
a present, Eeyore," Pooh said.
"It's a useful pot."

Eeyore picked up the balloon
and dropped it in the pot.

"Eeyore, I am glad I gave you
that pot," said Pooh.
"And I am glad
that I gave you something
to put into the pot,"
added Piglet.

Just then, Christopher Robin
and Eeyore's other friends
arrived.

Christopher Robin led them all
to Rabbit's house.

They had a birthday party for Eeyore.

Eeyore did not say much.

But he looked very, very happy.